Gumdrop
posts a
letter

Val Biro

CHILDRENS PRESS, CHICAGO

This Gumdrop book has been especially
drawn, and written in simple words
and sentences, for *Stepping Stones*.
Val Biro's many other Gumdrop stories
are available as full-size picture books.

Library of Congress Cataloging in Publication Data

Biro, Val, 1921-
  Gumdrop posts a letter.

  SUMMARY: Gumdrop the antique car helps the post
office van so that Mr. Oldcastle, his owner, can mail an
important letter.
  [1. Automobiles—Fiction] I. Title.
PZ7.B5233Gtp   [E]   76-50584
ISBN 0-516-03596-7

American edition published 1977 by
Regensteiner Publishing Enterprises, Inc.
All rights reserved. Printed in the U.S.A.
Published simultaneously in Canada.

Text and illustrations copyright © 1976 Val Biro
First published in 1976 by Knight Books and
Hodder & Stoughton Children's Books,
Salisbury Road, Leicester.
Printed and bound in Great Britain by Cox & Wyman Ltd.,
London, Fakenham and Reading.

U. S. 1962412

One day Mr. Oldcastle wrote
a letter. A most important letter
to his grandson Dan.

"I'd better run and post it,"
he said, and he ran to catch
the little red post office van.

3

"I say, wait for me!" he panted as he ran. But the postman didn't hear; he hopped into his van and drove away.

"And that's the last post today!" said Mr. Oldcastle. "But he can't have gone too far—I will stop him in my car!"

So he hopped in and drove after the van. "Gumdrop will catch the post," he said. "He is a good car, and better than most!"

A big red bus stood in the way.

"Have you seen the little red van?" he asked.

"Yes, man," said the driver, "he left the main road thataway!"

7

But now a truck barred
their way.

"Did you see the little red
van?" asked Mr. Oldcastle.

"Just about!" cried the man. "You'd better hurry! But will that old car stand the strain?"
"Gumdrop is better than most!" answered Mr. Oldcastle.

So he drove after the van. Just then they had to stop again. A crane was rattling down the lane.

What a host of trouble and pain!
"But we'll catch the post yet,"
said Mr. Oldcastle, and he drove on
when the coast was clear.

"Oh dear, he must be near," he
complained, as Gumdrop went
round and round. Then he saw a
tractor by the road.

"You're bound to catch him!" said the man. And there behind him went the little red van!

But all in vain. He lost the van again.
And then he saw a train.

"You can just catch him," said the
driver, "if you can get your old car up
that lane."

The lane was steep and Gumdrop
strained. So Mr. Oldcastle left the car
in gear, hopped out and helped it to the
top. Then he stopped and looked around.

And there below him was the
postman. He was looking at some cattle.
Gumdrop coasted down the lane.
"That'll catch him!" cried Mr. Oldcastle.

"I have a most important letter for my Dan," he said. "Please can you post it? It is on an urgent birthday matter."

"Nothing would please me better!" said the postman. He drove the little van off with a rattle.

"And now home again," said
Mr. Oldcastle.

But which way? They had come far
this day to post that letter. Then he saw
a sign.

"That's fine!" he cried. "That little
red van has led me round to the home
of my little boy Dan!"

And there was Dan.
"Grandad!" he called
as he ran to Gumdrop.
"Did you come for my
birthday?"

"No," said Mr. Oldcastle, "I just stopped in for a chat.

"As a matter of fact, I've just posted you a letter."

"Better and better!" said Dan
and they both laughed.